HUNGRY
COYOTE

HUNGRY
COYOTE

CHERYL BLACKFORD   *Illustrations by* **LAURIE CAPLE**

MINNESOTA HISTORICAL SOCIETY PRESS

www.mnhspress.org

The Minnesota Historical Society Press is a member of the Association of American University Presses.

Book design by Jen Schoeller, Mighty Media

Manufactured in the United States of America

10 9 8 7 6 5 4 3 2 1

♾ The paper used in this publication meets the minimum requirements of the American National Standard for Information Sciences—Permanence for Printed Library Materials, ANSI Z39.48-1984.

International Standard Book Number

ISBN: 978-0-87351-964-9 (cloth)

Library of Congress Cataloging-in-Publication Data
Blackford, Cheryl.
Hungry Coyote / Cheryl Blackford ; illustrations by Laurie Caple.
pages cm
Summary: "From winter hunts to picnic foraging, Coyote makes his deliberate way through the seasons in his urban habitat"— Provided by publisher.
ISBN 978-0-87351-964-9 (cloth : alk. paper)
1. Coyote—Juvenile fiction. [1. Coyote—Fiction. 2. Urban animals—Fiction. 3. Seasons—Fiction.] I. Caple, Laurie A., illustrator. II. Title.
PZ10.3.B5634Hun 2015
[E]—dc23
                              2014042450

The illustrator would like to thank Rick Hanestad and his family for the amazing opportunity to meet their charming, domesticated coyote, Wiley, and for sharing stories of his many antics.

For David, Eleanor, and Ben,
and the coyote by the lake.
C.B.

For Jim and Wiley
♥ L.C.

Down at the lake, the ice groans and thumps.

Sloppy snowflakes tumble and twirl,

clumping on hats, mittens, and eyelashes.

Children slip, slide, and glide.

Coyote slinks toward slick ice.

Wary and watchful, he sneaks past the crowd.

At the shore, voles scurry through secret tunnels. Coyote creeps between snow-frosted trees.

He listens, sniffs, and leaps.

Fwwwwoooomppppp

No vole for Coyote today.

No rabbits, mice, or squirrels either.

A bitter wind scours the lake.

Hungry Coyote howls for the spring.

Down at the lake, wind whips waves into frothy peaks.

Pale rays of sun warm the water. In the marsh, the frog orchestra tunes up. Children poke, dabble, and babble.

Coyote pads through boggy slop,
skirting the minnow seekers.

Near the shore, Coyote's mate gives birth
in their secret den.

Mrrrowwwlll

Six squirming pups whimper
and mewl for food.

Now Coyote hunts to feed his famished family.

He's on the prowl for plump rabbits,
meaty snakes, and slurpy turtle eggs.

A playful gust teases him with tempting scents.
Coyote dreams of summer feasts.

Down at the lake,

thunderclouds threaten.

The sky cracks open. Drenching rain beats
a pounding rhythm on docks and boats.

Children jump, twirl, and umbrella-whirl.

Coyote herds his playful pups
to shelter—safe from people
and the storm's fury.

At the shore, meat sizzles while picnickers play.

Coyote skulks until everyone leaves.

He drools, darts, and snatches.

Coyote grabs a greasy feast to share with his growing pups.

A brisk breeze sets leaves fluttering.
Coyote sniffs the first faint
perfume of fall.

Down at the lake, leaves swirl and spin.

Wind whirls autumn's litter into rustling piles. Frost nips at noses, ears, and toes. Children toss, tumble, and stumble.

Coyotes yip, yelp, and howl

Hawooooo

beneath the milky moon.

Near the shore, water birds snooze in feathery flocks. Shaggy shadows stalk, bounce, and pounce.

Splissshhh
Splassshhh
Flap

Birds fly from

needle-sharp teeth.

But one old goose will

feed the coyotes tonight.

A freezing squall brings fleeting
flurries. Coyote shakes droplets
from his winter coat.

Down at the lake,
new ice crackles
and snaps.

CITY COYOTES

Coyotes are smart, curious, and adaptable. They live on prairies, in forests, and on farmland. They even live in cities such as Minneapolis, Chicago, and New York. City coyotes might make their homes in parks or in nature preserves or on golf courses—all places where they can find plenty of food and shelter. Sometimes they live in small family groups, and sometimes they live alone.

What does a city coyote eat? Just about anything! They gobble up rodents such as rats, mice, and squirrels. They dine on rabbits, snakes, lizards, fish, and birds. They even munch on apples that fall from trees and steal vegetables from people's gardens. If you put out food for your dog or cat, they will eat that too. Never leave food or garbage where coyotes can find it. Instead, let them help us by eating pesky mice and rats.

You might never see a city coyote because they are shy—they usually travel at night to keep away from people. But you might hear one because coyotes are noisy creatures. They bark, yip, yelp, and howl to say, *I'm here. Where are you?* or, *If I don't know you, stay away.*

Some people are afraid of coyotes, but coyotes rarely bite people. If a coyote approaches you, don't run away. Instead, stand tall, wave your arms, and shout to frighten it away.

Coyotes are beautiful wild creatures.
We can enjoy sharing our cities with them.